Broken Sky

David R. Beshears

Large Print Edition

based on the screenplay
"Broken Sky"

Greybeard Publishing
Washington State

ISBN 978-0-9961818-2-2
(large print edition)

Greybeard Publishing
P.O. Box 480
McCleary, WA 98557-0480

Broken Sky

Prolog

The empty plain stretched out to the horizon. The alien sky overhead, awash in reds and purples, sat over the featureless landscape like a glass shell. The world was still and silent.

A sudden explosion of light and color and sound. The mountain range burst into existence, cutting across the panorama and replacing the thin thread of horizon with its jagged ridge line, a shadowy silhouette of dark blue.

Nestled in the mountains, at one end of a narrow valley, a smooth, gleaming white wall, set against a hillside, stood in contrast to the forest around it. A big man with sharp features and a hard gaze stood atop the wall, at the edge of an unadorned, flat rooftop. Karl lifted his gaze from the forest and out to the horizon, then above him to the reddish shell of sky overhead.

He appeared… satisfied.

Chapter One

Mannie Alvarez awoke in a small room of faded, roughhewn walls. A red shimmering glow pushed its way through the thin curtain that hung in the only window. He rose up from his cot, trudged over to an old sink and turned on the faucet. The pipes grumbled noisily, but the water came out clean.

Mannie was in his late thirties. His medium complexion hinted at a Hispanic heritage. He was a good looking man, but the life he had been living recently made him look tired all over.

He washed his face and hands, then walked through the narrow threshold between his bedroom and the main room of his two-room shack. He took a long, well-worn coat from its hook on the wall, put it on as he crossed the room and stepped out on a simple porch.

His shack was one of a dozen buildings that made up the tiny community. It had the appearance of a small, old-west town that had been dropped onto an alien world. The newly arrived mountain range was just visible as a dull shadow on the far horizon. The unearthly, cloudless sky above was a smear of reds and purples.

He watched a solitary figure in a hooded cloak walk across the street near the far end of town. Carla climbed the steps of the community hall and disappeared inside. After a few moments, Mannie stepped off his porch and started down the street.

The front room of the community hall was cluttered with several couches, small end tables and coffee tables, and a couple of round dining tables. It was lit by a handful of oil lamps sitting on tables and hanging on walls. Nothing in the room matched, as if it had all been collected haphazardly over time.

Mannie took off his coat and hung it beside Carla's cloak.

There were several other people in the room. Some glanced up at Mannie before returning to whatever they had been doing; most did not.

Yolanda Yates was a black woman in her early fifties. She wore khaki trousers and a heavy shirt; her hair was pulled back tight and bound in a bun.

The General was in his sixties. His short hair was gray around the ears, salt and pepper on top. His clothes, despite being civilian, hung on him as if they had a military cut.

Ben, a young boy of about nine, was playing a game of checkers with Professor Westin, a tall, thin man in his late sixties. The Professor's graying hair looked as though it used to be neat and trim, but had since grown shaggy.

Carla was standing before a small, tattered chalk board. She erased the number "21" that had been written on it, carefully wrote "22". Setting the piece of chalk back in the tray, she glanced silently at Mannie. She was in her early forties, and in a different life would have been considered attractive.

She turned about and disappeared through the door beside the chalk board.

Young Ben looked up from the checker game as Mannie started across the room. He spoke softly so as not to disturb the muffled hush that lay over the room.

"Mrs. Johansen says breakfast will be ready any minute."

"Thanks, Ben." Mannie followed Carla through the door.

Carla was at the counter mixing up a pitcher of milk.

Mrs. Johansen stood at a wood-burning cook stove, looking down into a pot of oatmeal. She had the look and dress of a middle-aged pioneer woman, strong but weathered by a harsh life.

"Good morning, Mannie," she said.

"How are you this morning, Mrs. Johansen?"

"The oatmeal will be ready in a minute," she said. "We could use more wood for the stove."

Mannie picked up the empty basket beside the back door. Stepping outside, he let the door swing slowly closed behind him.

The back walls of the buildings to either side of the community hall were lined up with that of the hall. Looking outward, the landscape ahead was wide open. No buildings, no trees, nothing.

Mannie walked over to a scattering of cut and split firewood that lay strewn about on the ground; all that remained of the wood pile. He knelt down and picked up the few scraps, tossed them one by one into the basket.

He heard the sound of the door opening and saw Carla step outside. She stood silently near the door, glanced once at Mannie before turning her attention to the barren landscape.

Mannie picked up the basket, walked slowly over to her and set the basket down beside her.

Carla folded her arms across her chest, glanced again at Mannie, again looked away and stared out across the landscape. The quiet was oppressive. The tiny cluster of buildings and the handful of people living in the small community were utterly alone in the alien isolation.

Mannie could see Carla's apprehension, the thinly veiled look of concern on her face. He didn't ask her what was bothering her. He turned away, tried to ignore her unease.

Young Ben burst through the door. "They're back!"

Mannie gave Carla a quick, heartening smile and started toward the corner of the building, disappeared between the community hall and the building beside it.

Those who had been in the community hall now stood out in the dusty street in front of the building, their attention focused up the road.

Two figures were visible in the distance, approaching on foot. John Devon was pulling a small cart, Robin Hanley walking beside it.

Devon looked like someone plucked out of middle-America; white, late thirties, a wife and two-point-five children waiting for him in a three bedroom home somewhere in a quiet, middle-class neighborhood in a quiet, middle-class community.

Robin was in her early twenties, but could pass for a teenager. Her long, medium brown hair was pulled back into a ponytail.

Both looked as though they had been on a long trek.

They drew nearer, and at some unseen signal those who had been waiting rushed forward to greet them. Within moments, the new arrivals were surrounded by relieved friends who began bombarding them with "we thought we'd lost you…", "Are we ever glad to see you…", and most notably "what'd you find?"

Mannie remained outside the group and waited. Devon eventually left the cart and pushed his way through the crowd. Approaching Mannie, he shook head in a silent 'no'.

Mannie indicated that they should walk. The two started toward the alleyway between the two buildings opposite the community hall.

"Wish I had better news," said Devon.

"Not one to get my hopes up."

"We did come across two new creeks, a grove of trees. That's about it."

Once through the alley, they continued on toward a wooden water tank sitting on a raised platform seven feet above the ground. A hand pump brought water up from a well and into the tank. A hose wound down one of the corner posts to a faucet.

Devon set his pack down and turned on the faucet. They continued to talk as he washed up.

"We went ten days out before turning back. I swear, those mountains never got an inch closer. How is that possible? I mean, no matter how far away they are, shouldn't they have appeared closer after ten days march?"

"In the real world, maybe," said Mannie. "You brought back wood, anyway."

"We stopped at that grove of trees on the way back." The wood would be green, but there wasn't much seasoned firewood left. It was better than nothing.

Devon finished washing. He took an old, worn towel from its hook near the faucet and began to dry his face and hands. "Where the hell are we, Mannie? What is this place?"

"Wrong guy to ask… I don't even know who *you* are." *I don't know who any of you are*.

It was a welcome home celebration. Two tables were set up in the main street, and all ten residents of the community were there.

Lee Takahashi, a middle-aged Asian man with a pleasant face, friendly eyes and a calm smile had missed that morning's return, having been on a short foraging trip in the other direction. His half-day excursion had netted the group a handful of potatoes and a small, wooden box.

There was a bustling of activity as the residents passed dishes of food back and forth, speaking animatedly to one another in lighthearted voices. The food was lacking in quantity and color and variety. There was a pot of thin stew, a serving plate containing something gray and mashed that was most likely the potatoes that Lee had brought back, a basket of pale colored bread rolls, and a pitcher of watered down powdered milk.

Mrs. Johansen stood in front of the pot of stew. She began filling bowls and passing them down.

"Looks like we'll all be sleeping with full bellies tonight," the General said cheerfully, setting his bowl down in front of him.

Devon held up his glass of milk. "I thank everyone for this fine welcome home." He took a drink as others held their glasses out in toast.

"We're glad that you and Robin are home safe, Mr. Devon," said Mrs. Johansen.

Robin sighed contentedly. "Everything looks delicious."

"And it tastes magnificent," said the General. "Well done, Mrs. Johansen."

"Thank you, General." Mrs. Johansen nodded to Lee Takahashi. "And the potatoes should round out the meal quite nicely."

Lee nodded politely.

Mannie studiously watched as those around the two tables began spooning their stew, taking bites of their rolls, and scooping up their small portions of mashed potatoes. Conversations grew more muffled as everyone began eating in earnest.

Half an hour later, Mannie stood near the community hall porch observing the after-dinner activity going on at the tables. Devon and the Professor moved away from the others and started in his direction. He acknowledged their approach with an easy nod and a soft-spoken greeting.

"Waddya say, Professor?"

The Professor took a drink from a faded plastic cup before answering. "I say that despite efforts to the contrary, I am anticipating an increasing state of hunger amongst the populace."

"A distinct possibility."

Devon smirked. "You're dampening the happy mood, Professor."

"Mood be damned," said the Professor. Then in a softer tone, "I understand we have serious matters to discuss." When Mannie and Devon said nothing, the Professor pushed ahead. "We're going to have to send out another team."

This time, Mannie managed to give a noncommittal shrug.

The Professor frowned. "What other choice is there?"

"I doubt it's going to be enough."

"Then what are you suggesting we do?"

"You know what he's suggesting," said Devon.

With that, the Professor frowned and let out a low growl. He looked over at the group gathered around the tables, then turned back and looked sharply at Devon and Mannie.

"You're talking about abandoning the town."

"It's an option," said Mannie.

Devon nodded. "It's already being talked about."

"Where would we go?"

"To the mountains," Mannie stated flatly.

"Mr. Devon has already tried that," said the Professor.

"The mountain range is there," said Mannie. "We can see it."

"We just can't get to it."

"Of course we can."

Devon threw Mannie's earlier words back at him. "In the real world, maybe."

Mannie smirked at that, but the Professor was not amused. He gave Devon a stern, professorial look.

"Can we reach it or not, Mr. Devon?"

"I don't know," Devon said, after a long pause. "But we're going to have to try something, and we're going to have to try it soon."

The three of them stood silent then. They all knew that something had to change. The Professor finally nodded in the direction of the General, who was holding court over by the dinner tables.

"What does the General have to say?" he asked.

"I haven't talked to him about it," said Mannie.

Devon sounded doubtful. "I don't think he's all that keen on leaving."

"He's been here longer than any of us," said the Professor, "and he has experiences to draw on that none of the rest of us have."

"Hey, I'm not all that keen on leaving town either," said Mannie. "If he has another option, I'd be interested in hearing what it is."

"Good," said the Professor. He spoke then to both of them. "I agree that our situation is growing increasingly dire. We must have a stable food supply. And, yes, our time to take action is limited. As our existing stores diminish, any such action may become more difficult."

Over at the tables, the others of the group were in light, animated conversation; stark contrast to their surroundings and the mood of the three at the steps of the community hall.

It was nearing dusk, and the strange colors in the sky were growing darker. Mannie worked the pump handle beneath the water tank, bringing water up from the well and drawing it into the tank above him. It was a regular chore that usually fell to him or Devon.

He saw Carla approaching, kept pumping even after she reached him and looked silently down at him.

"Is another team going out?" she finally asked.

"I suppose." His tone was matter-of-fact. He kept working the pump. He could hear the water being drawn up through the pipe and into the tank.

"Supplies are low," said Carla.

"I know that."

"People are getting nervous."

"I know that, too."

Carla wrapped her arms around herself, looked around them in frustration. She frowned then. "Are we going to abandon the town?"

Mannie straightened, locked down the pump handle. He looked as though he had just finished a round at the gym.

"Not my decision, Carla."

"That's not what I asked."

"Yeah, well, it's all I have."

"Yeah, *well*, it's not good enough." Carla gave him a sharp glare. "You know what it was like before we had the town. As bad as things are, this is better than… *out there*."

"Like I said. Not my decision."

Carla was about to respond with a carefully thought out biting retort when something caught her attention. She turned away from Mannie. He sensed it then as well. He looked around them, then looked to the sky. The both looked to the sky…

The sky darkened. The faint breeze that had been blowing stopped.

The world held its breath.

The Professor stood on the porch of the community hall. He was looking up at the same sky as Mannie and Carla. Mrs. Johansen came outside and stood beside him.

The sky exploded in blinding light and color. It lasted for several heartbeats. There was a deep, resonating boom.

And then it was over. The two standing on the porch listened and waited.

"West?" Mrs. Johansen suggested, breaking the brief silence.

"North, I think," answered the Professor. "Any guesses as to what we might find, Mrs. Johansen?"

"Pray it's food, Professor."

"Think big, madam. A restaurant. A roadside establishment that serves decadently large portions."

Back at the water tank, Mannie and Carla were looking to the north.

"North again," said Carla.

"Looks like it." Mannie started walking back to the cluster of buildings that was home. Carla followed beside him. They moved casually, as if nothing had happened.

"Sure hope it's food," said Carla. "A long way off, though."

"Couple a' days at least."

It was morning, an hour or so past dawn; or what passed for dawn. Mannie walked from his bedroom into the main room of his shack, carrying a partially filled canvas pack in one hand, a balled-up shirt in the other. He set the pack onto a small table and stuffed the shirt into it.

Devon stepped into the open front doorway from the porch.

"I wish ya luck."

Mannie walked over to a shelf and picked up a small, leather pouch. He returned to the table and continued packing. He gave a muffled grunt of a thank you.

"Yeah," Devon mumbled back. "You sure you don't want me to go with you?"

Mannie lifted the pack over one shoulder. "You just got back. We'll be fine." He started toward the door and Devon backed out to give him room.

Out on the porch, they could see the wooden cart parked in front of the community hall. A small group had gathered around it.

"You sure you want to take the General?" asked Devon.

"Tough old bird is gonna outlive us all," said Mannie.

"You know that's not what I meant."

Mannie's grin broadened as he stepped down into the street. Devon followed after him and they started in the direction of the others.

"You should probably start making plans," Mannie stated flatly.

"I am."

"Whatever we find on this trip, if anything, won't make a bit of difference in the long run."

"But in the short run, we may get something to eat," Devon said calmly. "Who knows, maybe a change of clothes?"

This time, Mannie's grin wasn't quite as broad. "And that's why I'm going." He lost all humor. "You and I both know there's not enough coming in to sustain us. We stay, we starve."

"You really think you can convince everyone to leave?"

"Their choice. They can leave or stay." Mannie looked side-glance at Devon. "What about you?"

"Oh, I'm convinced we can't stay." He nodded in the general direction of the purple silhouette on the horizon. "I'm not convinced that we'll ever reach those mountains."

Mannie looked back to the crowd they were approaching. "Not my place to make anyone leave. Anyone wants to stay, I got no quarrel. That includes you."

"But you're going." It was a statement. There was no question in the tone.

"Planning on it. Unless the General has something up his sleeve."

They reached the others and Mannie tossed his pack into the back of the cart. Devon held his hand out and he and Mannie shook hands.

"We should be back in a week," said Mannie.

"I'll see what I can do." Devon stepped back. So did several others. The General started around toward the front of the cart, and Carla and Lee Takahashi followed.

"Let's get at it," Mannie said to the General, and the two of them began pulling the cart, Carla and Lee walking beside them.

The Professor and Ben stood in the middle of the dirt street and watched the search team pull away. The others drifted slowly in the direction of the community hall.

They switched out every few hours, Mannie and the General pulling the cart for a while, then Carla and Lee Takahashi. The wheels rolled smoothly over the flat plain of short, yellow grass, the landscape stretching away unchanged all the way to the horizon, where the mountain range was little more than a purple smudge. The sky overhead was as alien in appearance as always, but away from the town it seemed all the more artificial, like a colorful dome set into place over them.

After a short break for lunch, Carla and Lee took up cart duty, following the General and Mannie who walked twenty paces ahead of them.

"What are you hoping we'll find, Lee?" asked Carla. They estimated they were two days from the materialization site.

"We find what we find, Miss Masterson." Lee Takahashi didn't talk much, and when he did, he kept his comments brief.

"Very profound, *Mr. Takahashi*, but there must be something that, if you could ask for anything, would be waiting for us up there."

Lee gave it thought. "Then," he stated succinctly, "I would wish for shoes for the boy."

"Shoes?"

"Yes."

"That's it… Shoes for Ben…"

"The boy needs shoes."

"Hmm," she said softly. "That's cool." She turned her attention back to the task of pulling the cart. "But then, why not wish for a whole crate of shoes?"

"Because he does not need a whole crate of shoes."

And with that, they trudged forward in silence.

By midday the following day, most of those in the group were growing increasingly ill at ease, though perhaps not all for the same reason.

Lee and Carla, walking some distance ahead, said nothing to each other. This was to be expected of Lee, but it was surprising that Carla said nothing.

The General and Mannie were taking their turn at the cart. The General had been talking about one thing or another for over an hour, leaving Mannie to half listen and free to let his mind wander.

Eventually even the General fell into an uncomfortable quiet. After more than a dozen steps, his silence began to make Mannie feel uneasy. He was about to ask the General whether there was something bothering him when the older man spoke up.

"I believe we should have reached the site by now, Mr. Alvarez."

"We haven't missed it, General," said Mannie.

"And to what do you attribute such confidence?"

At that very moment, Carla turned her head and called out to them. "Something up ahead," she said.

Mannie fought down a grin. "To an unfailing sense of direction, General."

Fifteen minutes later Mannie and the General drew the cart to a stop. Carla and Lee were already walking carefully around and through a number of items scattered about the site.

Among the debris was an office chair, a wooden desk, and a small side table. Carla gave the chair a slow spin as she walked past it.

Lee squatted down and picked a book up from a pile lying on the ground and began paging through it.

The General moved away from the cart, took several steps forward, stopped and glanced down at several binders that were lying on the ground. One lay open, papers fluttering in the slight breeze. He stood with his hands clasped behind his back. "What do we have, Miss Masterson?" he asked.

"It could be better, General."

The General studied what appeared to be the remains of an office. "We can dismantle the furniture for fuel," he said. "If no one needs the items, of course."

"I think we already have all the office furniture we can use," said Mannie.

Lee stood then, tossed the book that he had been looking at back onto the pile. "I don't think much of the gentleman's reading habits."

"Your opinion notwithstanding, Mr. Takahashi," said the General, "I would imagine the previous occupant of this office might miss his reference materials."

"These reference materials have nothing to do with business, General."

It took a moment, but the General finally realized what Lee Takahashi was inferring.

"Ah. I see."

Mannie watched Carla approach the desk. "Anything in the desk?" he asked her.

She rummaged through the drawers, mumbling the names of the items she found. Pencils, pens, notepads… She opened a side drawer, pulled out a portfolio and set it on the desktop. She opened it, pulled out a business card and read it silently. She spoke then as she tucked it back into the portfolio.

"Mister James Barstow, from Jackson, Oregon; an accountant, apparently."

Mannie raised a brow. "How exciting for him."

The General continued his survey of the relocated office. "His life has no doubt recently grown a tad more stimulating."

Carla sighed noisily. "At least the poor guy wasn't sitting at his desk when it suddenly vanished from Jackson, Oregon."

"You see anything else?" asked Mannie.

Carla flipped through several pages that were tucked into the side pocket of the portfolio. "Nothing much. Except… these all have dates from about two years ago."

"Interesting," said Lee.

"But what does it mean?" asked Mannie.

"It could mean any number of things," said Lee. "But it is interesting."

The General spoke in a smooth, observational tone. "How so, sir? We have previously collected things that have to all appearances come from other times."

"*Appeared to*," Lee noted. "We find a piece of furniture made thirty years in the past, it may have come from thirty years ago, but it may have come from any time since it was originally manufactured. This is more definitive. Our friend Mr. Barstow isn't likely to carry letters all dated two years ago and nothing sooner, nothing later."

Mannie stepped over to the pile of books that Lee had been looking at and started rummaging through them. He opened one, checked something on one of the first few pages, tossed it aside and looked at another, then another.

"Copyright dates correspond to the letters. Some older, but none newer than two years ago."

The General nodded curtly at that, then surveyed the scene around them.

"Information that we may be able to use down the road," he said. "I suggest that we gather what supplies we may be able to use—writing materials, wood for our fires, and so on. We have a three day journey home."

The little town was awash in muted evening colors. Mannie crossed the street and approached the community hall. Climbing the steps up to the porch, he could hear the low rumbling of conversation going on inside.

All the residents of the community were gathered in the main room, a few standing, the rest sitting in the mismatched couches and chairs.

"Good evening, sir," said the General.

"General." Mannie took the one step down into the room. He nodded at Lee, who was standing out of the way, his back against the far wall.

"We were just discussing our options," said the Professor.

"And what have you come up with?" asked Mannie.

Carla spoke up in a calm monotone. "We can leave, or we can stay."

The Professor smiled patiently. "If we leave, there is the small matter of where to go. Do we go to the mountains? Or perhaps somewhere else? If we stay, do we choose to stay indefinitely? Do we set a timetable or some other milestone before choosing to leave?"

"And what is the consensus?"

Devon piped in. "We haven't gotten that far."

"What if we don't reach a consensus?" asked Carla. "Do some go and some stay?"

"Each chooses their own path," Mannie stated coolly.

The light coming in through the window continued to grow dim. Mrs. Johansen set about to turn on the lamps. The Professor watched her for several moments before turning his attention to the group as a whole.

"I believe that prior to a decision being made, we should hear the General's views on the matter."

"Waddya' say, General?" Devon asked almost cheerily. "You've been unusually quiet."

The General stared straight ahead, giving away nothing of what he might be thinking, but looking as though he was gathering his thoughts.

The Professor tried to encourage him.

"You have been here longer than any of us," he said. "You've seen things that none of us have seen. You were the first to find this town, back when it was just three buildings and nothing else."

"None of that gives me more insight than any of you as to what we should do."

"Nonetheless, I would very much value your opinion, General."

"I appreciate that, Professor." The General shifted position, seemed to look inward. "I have watched our community grow; watched as each of you, in turn, found your way here and found some solace in residing within a collection of boxes with windows and doors… and chose to stay.

"And yes, I have seen some things out there, things quite extraordinary, even by the standards of where we now find ourselves. I have no doubt that all of you have witnessed things just as unusual as any that I have seen."

The General grew quiet. The others waited, and when he spoke again, he was very introspective. "This is not a world in which to be alone. The isolation can be quite overwhelming."

"You were alone a long time," said Carla.

"Yes, Ma'am. About four years, best I can figure. Maybe three years out there, another year here in town." The General turned to the boy. "And then you showed up, son. I haven't had a moment's peace since."

The boy grinned. The Professor watched and waited for what he believed to be a politely appropriate amount of time. "So what do we do, General?"

"I don't believe we have a choice, Professor."

"Are you suggesting that we leave?"

"We are seeing far fewer of the materializations, at least within a reasonable distance of town. Of those we can reach, we are finding less and less food."

"But to just leave..." said Carla, almost pleading.

"I don't like the idea any more than you, Miss Masterson." Such as it was, this collection of broken down old buildings had become home. For all of them.

Robin Hanley, who had spoken very little throughout the meeting, leaned forward, crossed her arms and held her elbows in her hands. "Where would be go?"

"Yes, General," the Professor said firmly. "Do you recommend the mountains, as Mannie has suggested? Or do you share the concerns that several others have voiced? That they cannot be reached..."

"They can be reached. They are like any other materialization."

"A mountain range is more than a couch," said Carla.

The General tiredly shook his head. "There was nothing there, girl. Then there was a crack in the sky, and the mountains fell through."

There was a long moment of silence before Mannie said softly, "Just like a couch."

The dull gray light that had been coming in through the window had continued to fade until now there was only darkness beyond the glass. The few lamps in the room glowed yellow, pushing shadows across the already darkened faces of the group.

Chapter Two

Carla stood just inside Mannie's open front door, the alien world behind her bathed in darkness. She saw his familiar canvas bag on the table, now half full. There was a small wooden crate beside him, once used to carry fruit, of late used to hold Mannie's few possessions.

Mannie came into the room from the bedroom, rolling up his blanket as he walked over to the table. He saw Carla standing in the doorway, but said nothing.

"You aren't taking much," said Carla.

"Not much to take." Mannie placed the tightly rolled blanket into the wood-slated box. Studying the canvas bag and the crate a moment, he finally picked up the bag and set it into the box with the odds and ends. "Not much more than I came with," he said thoughtfully.

"You have a roof over your head."

"I won't argue this with you, Carla." Mannie looked frustrated and slightly annoyed. "I'm not in charge here. I'm not ordering anyone to go."

"But we are going, though, aren't we?"

"You can stay."

"No. I can't."

Mannie picked up his box and started toward the door. "I'm sorry."

Outside, the shell of the predawn sky overhead was a deep, dark blue. In front of the community hall, the cart was nearly filled with assorted boxes, bags, long-handled tools, and other supplies. Lee Takahashi was methodically shifting the contents about, attempting to make more room.

Robin Hanley stood to one side, wrapped tightly in a long blanket. She didn't appear all that comfortable with recent events.

As Mannie approached the cart, Lee spoke without looking up from work.

"I'll take that."

Mannie handed him his box. "Need any help?"

"I just about have it."

Devon stepped out of the community hall and onto the porch, carrying a box of pans and metal plates.

"Nice timing, old boy." He climbed down the steps and handed the box to Lee. "That's the last of it, Lee." He turned then and gave a despondent look in the direction of the porch just as Mrs. Johansen stepped through the door. "The General was right, Ma'am. This is no place to be alone."

"Thanks just the same, Mr. Devon," said Mrs. Johansen. "Out there… that's not for me."

"What we've left for you won't last long."

"You've left me more than my share."

Mannie approached the foot of the steps. "You know the direction we've taken, if you change your mind."

Robin wrapped herself more tightly in the blanket. "We'll be watching for you."

Mrs. Johansen gave Robin a gentle smile, said nothing more.

Devon gave up and turned away, moved around to the front of the cart, to where Lee was waiting. The General stepped out ahead and led the way as Lee and Devon began pulling the loaded cart. Ben and the Professor followed behind.

Robin stood silent in the center of the street. Carla looked up again at Mrs. Johansen, suddenly rushed up the steps and the two women hugged.

Mannie and Yolanda waited at the base of the steps.

"They've been together a long time, those two," said Yolanda. "I'm surprised Carla is leaving without her."

"She hasn't left yet," Mannie mumbled.

Yolanda gave Mannie a parental smirk. Carla and Mrs. Johansen reluctantly pulled apart and Carla took the steps down from the porch. She gave Mannie a hard look as she passed him and followed the others. Mannie and Yolanda followed a safe distance behind.

Robin had yet to move from her spot in the middle of the dirt road. She continued to look up at Mrs. Johansen, who remained stoic on the community hall porch.

"Go, child," the woman said, and gave Robin a reassuring nod.

Robin turned finally and slowly trailed after the others.

The travelers sat in a circle on the ground beside the cart. The night sky was a dark blue, with no stars, but there was a glow to it that illuminated the smooth surface of the plain and lay over the group. Some had finished their dinner, and their empty metal plates were on the ground beside them. Some held metal cups in hand. The conversation was light.

Yolanda looked out on the emptiness that surrounded them. "It's always so quiet out here," she said. "I think that's what bothers me the most. Not the weird sky or the fear of going hungry, or even the arrivals. It's too quiet. It's not right. It's not normal."

"There's nothing normal about this place," said Devon. He sat with his back against one wheel of the cart.

The Professor set his cup down beside his empty plate. "Tell us, Miss Yates, what did you do back in the real world, before you were snatched away and brought here?"

Yolanda put on a sheepish expression and didn't answer right away. Seeing this, Devon grinned.

"This must be good," he said. "And why have we never heard your story before?"

"Come now, Mr. Devon," said the Professor, stepping in to defend Yolanda, using his most fatherly tone. "As our most recent resident, we must give Miss Yates time to grow comfortable enough to tell us her tale."

"She's been with us quite long enough, Professor. We've all told our life stories... *ad nauseam*. It's long past time for something fresh."

"I don't mind," said Yolanda. "I just don't have much reason to talk about it."

"And so?"

"I... told fortunes."

"Ya what?"

The Professor pursed his lips. "I see."

"For the tourists," Yolanda stated more firmly. "I did rather well."

"Monetarily, or…?" asked Devon.

"The money."

"Hmm," the Professor sighed.

"Tourists expected to see a black woman in full regalia dispensing fortunes. They went home feeling like they got what they came for."

"Of course." The Professor changed the direction of the conversation. "Where were you when you were taken?"

"At the breakfast table, in the back room of my store. I was eating a bowl of cereal."

"A pleasant memory, then?"

"I enjoyed the quiet time before the day got noisy," said Yolanda. There was a hint of nostalgia in her voice. "I guess I didn't really know what quiet was."

There was a long pause then, before Yolanda came out of her reverie. "How about you, Professor? What of your exit from the real world? I don't suppose you were standing in front of your class, to suddenly vanish from the podium, leaving your students befuddled?"

"Nothing so dramatic, I'm afraid. I was in my office, grading papers."

Devon repositioned himself, finding a more comfortable spot against the cart wheel. "I didn't know professors did that any more. I thought they left that to assistants."

"I like to get my hands dirty, every now and then, Mr. Devon." The Professor managed to speak down to Devon, as a Professor softly giving a student a verbal slap on the wrist.

Yolanda turned to Devon. "How about you, John? What were you doing when you were taken?"

Mannie, who had been listening to the conversation from a distance, chuckled lightly. Devon gave him a disapproving look before answering.

"Well," he muttered, "as most of you know, I was in the shower."

It took a moment for Yolanda to realize what that meant. When she did, she tried not to appear startled, but the surprise was evident in her tone and expression.

"You came here naked?"

Mannie answered for Devon. "Bare-assed and baby fresh."

Devon grumbled. "Shampoo in my hair."

"Oh my," said Yolanda.

The entire group grew quiet, staring out at nothing in particular. Most had slight smiles, thinking on Devon disappearing from his shower, arriving here, out on the open plain, wet and soapy.

Then came the realization that Devon's situation hadn't been funny at all. No food or water was bad enough; but no clothes…

And the smiles faded.

"Oh my," Yolanda said again.

And the smiles slowly returned. And then light laughter from those sitting around the glow of the lantern.

Lucas stood unseen in the shadows beyond the camp, observing the group gathered in a circle around the lantern, the cart parked to one side. The glow of the light from the sky overhead illuminated the landscape just enough to distinguish his features. He was in his twenties, slim and small featured, below average in height. There was the hint of a boyish appearance about him.

He watched the group; intent, focused. His attention wasn't menacing, but there was something ominous about his gaze.

The sounds of laughter reached out to him. A slight smile shown on his face.

Back in the camp, a curious, unsettled look crossed Yolanda's face. The smile born from the laughter moments earlier slowly faded.

She turned her head, looked beyond the camp. She looked in the direction of the unseen observer standing in the shadows just beyond the reach of the light.

She saw nothing. And yet…

"Yolanda?" asked Devon. "What is it?"

Yolanda gazed out beyond the camp a few moments longer, shook her head uncertainly.

"I don't know," she said softly. She turned back finally to the others, tried to bring back her smile, but now it was forced. "It's nothing… Like I said, it's too quiet out here."

In the shadows beyond the camp, Lucas hadn't moved. He watched, studied. There was a sparkle in his eye; a reflection from the glow reaching out from the camp.

The group started out again a little after dawn the next morning, taking two hour shifts at the cart, always marching in the direction of the smudge of silhouette on the horizon. The day passed as the day before, and the next passed as the day before that.

Five days, each like the one before it. Late afternoon; the Professor and the General were pulling the cart. Mannie and Lee were several hundred feet out in front, with the rest trailing behind.

Carla and young Ben walked together. They talked some of their lives before coming to this strange place, particularly about the people they had known. Ben spoke of his family. Carla had heard it all before, but she responded as if she was hearing it for the first time.

The conversation eventually came around to the woman they had left back in town, now all alone.

"I wouldn't worry about Mrs. Johansen, Ben. She's a tough lady. She got along well enough before she met up with the rest of us."

"Yeah, but times are different," said Ben. "That's why we left, isn't it?"

"Yes, that's true," said Carla. "But now she only has herself to care for. She doesn't have to mother hen all of us."

Up ahead, Lee and Mannie had been walking in silence since they took over point almost two hours earlier. Neither was all that adept at making light conversation.

Now, Lee Takahashi began making subtle facial expressions as if he intended to speak. He finally cleared his throat.

"Mr. Alvarez," he began, then paused.

Mannie waited for Lee to continue, finally urged him on. "Yeah?"

"Mannie," Lee began again, pushing ahead. "Perhaps we should consider going to three-quarter rations."

"We need all our energy, Lee."

"We're going through our supplies more quickly than anticipated."

Mannie's brow scrunched up in thought. "We figured we had what, fourteen days?"

"Yes. And after five days, we have consumed at least half of our rations."

"That's not so bad, really."

"The mountains are no closer."

"They're closer," said Mannie. "They just don't look closer."

"Of course," Lee said patiently. "My mistake."

"We shouldn't expect to see them any closer for at least another five days, maybe more. We know that much from Devon's trip."

"I understand that," said Lee. "It is for that reason that I believe we need to begin conserving our supplies. If we do not, we will be out of food long before we reach the mountains; even by your own estimations."

Lee and Mannie marched forward in silence for several long seconds. Mannie stared straight ahead, in the general direction of the bluish silhouette of the mountain range.

"All right," he said at last. *Damn. He's right.* "Three-quarter rations."

The General and the Professor were walking point, Carla and Yolanda pulling the cart ten paces behind. Far behind the cart, the others marched in pairs.

The General looked slightly to the left. Something caught his eye. At least, he thought so. He said nothing, but continued glancing to the left as he and the Professor continued trudging forward.

A shadow appeared in the distance a few degrees off the direction in which they were marching. The shadow slowly formed into the shape of a man.

The General caught the Professor's attention and indicated the figure coming toward them.

The Professor nodded and they continued walking. Behind them, the rest of the group quietly followed, with only the sound of the cart's wheels turning on their axles breaking the silence.

Details formed on the silhouette and they could see then that the man was Mannie. They continued ahead for several more minutes before stopping to let Mannie finish closing the distance, settling in for a break.

When Mannie reached them, he let his pack slide down from his shoulder and tossed it into the cart. "There's a gorge two days ahead," he said. "Cuts right across our path."

"Now what?" asked Carla.

"We go to the gorge."

"And then what?"

Mannie turned in the direction he had just come from. The only thing visible was the mountain range, looking exactly as it always had.

"You can't see it until you get right up to it," he said. "But down inside, it's like a forest."

"Water?" asked the General. Water was in very short supply.

"Has to be. I didn't go down, but I did find what may be the only route." He gave a curt nod. "And from the gorge, the mountains look closer. A lot closer."

Mannie and Devon approached the edge of the gorge. It appeared as a deep gash in the earth; in the distance far beyond, the mountains were indeed visibly closer, if only a little.

They stepped to the very edge of the precipice and looked down. A cool breeze rose up to brush across their faces. The gorge below was filled with dark green forest, the canopy far below the lip of the canyon-like walls. The only sound was that of the cart coming up behind them as the rest of the group drew nearer.

"Okay," said Devon, breaking the silence. "Not something you see every day." He stretched out beyond the edge, studied the sheer walls below them. "Where's this way down?"

Mannie nodded to their left. "That way; not far." He looked back at the others, now only a matter of yards away. "We'll have to leave the cart. Carry what we can."

Once everyone had a chance to have a look at the wide chasm that cut across their path, they turned and started along the edge. It took only a few minutes to find the way down, such as it was; a switchback trail never more than two feet wide, often much narrower.

It took some time to sort through the supplies and decide what to take and what to leave behind, but eventually everyone had a full pack and they started down. Perhaps they could come back some day and collect up what remained, most likely not.

Mannie led the way down the canyon wall. They found themselves slipping and sliding as much as walking and climbing. The forest canopy was far below, an indication of the depth of the gorge and just how far they had to descend.

Midway down, with the treetops still some distance below, the sky above exploded in a violent storm of wind and light and color. It was as if the *materialization* was opening up right there amongst them. Half the group lost their footing and began sliding. Those that managed to stop themselves grasped and held onto those sliding past.

Once the world around them had once again quieted, Carla steadied herself. "That was…" she started, but was unable to finish.

Lee Takahashi spoke in a matter-of-fact tone. "I believe there was an arrival quite near here."

"Ya think?"

"An arrival?" Ben asked anxiously. "Right here?"

"Very near," said Lee.

Those below Carla began moving again. "We'll be all right, Ben," she said, and once again started the descent. "We just need to keep moving."

The Professor continued to see things from an academic perspective. "This entire gorge is no doubt the result of materializations; the forest as well."

"Thanks for that, Professor," Carla said sardonically.

The rest of the climb down was quiet. The trail, such as it was, wound back and forth, sometimes quite steep, at other times an easy descent.

Mannie reached the floor and stepped away from the foot of the cliff wall. The clearing at the base was narrow, and opposite the wall stood a nearly impenetrable growth of trees and brush. As Mannie studied the vegetation for the best route in, the others gathered behind him one at a time as they reached the floor.

"Oh, man," said Devon, dreading going into the brush even more than he had dreaded the climb down.

"Well put, Mr. Devon," said the Professor.

Mannie turned his head slightly and looked first at Devon, then at the Professor.

Carla, however, spoke up first. "Well?"

"Onward then?" suggested the Professor.

"Let's get at it," said Mannie. He started forward, pushing into the brush where it looked most accessible. There was no trail that they could find, but the way was passable. Mannie used his sense of direction, which was in fact better than most, but they also managed to capture glimpses of the far wall of the gorge now and then whenever the trees thinned out enough to give them a clear view.

An hour after reaching the gorge floor they came to a meandering brook. They stopped to fill canteens and water bags, and rested for a while, before again pushing on. They stopped again at midday when they came to a clearing. Packs rested where they were dropped.

The General drank from a leather water bag, and handed it to Lee.

"How far do you estimate?" he asked Lee.

"Not long now." Lee put the cap back on the water bag and handed it back.

The Professor stepped out of the woods, having taken care of business. "One step forward, two steps back," he said. "I feel we may be going backward."

"I believe that we have, once or twice," said Lee.

At that moment, the sky suddenly turned very dark, followed seconds later by flashes of light and explosive booms.

The Professor looked at Lee with some concern. Devon looked over at Mannie, who tried to appear calm but was clearly unsettled.

The moment passed. The world grew quiet once again.

"That's the fourth arrival since we've been here," said Carla.

Third, actually, thought Lee. "I believe that with each, the forest grows thicker," he said.

Ben said aloud what everyone was thinking. "What happens if an arrival happens here? Right here?"

After several seconds during which no one answered, Yolanda stood up.

"Let's not find out," she said flatly. She picked up her pack and began to slip into it. Others came to their feet. Everyone was up then and picking up their gear, although most were deliberately calm about it.

They spent another hour struggling through heavy undergrowth beneath the thick forest canopy. The line of travelers stretched through the brush, Mannie continuing in the lead, making a rough path for the others to follow.

There was an explosive boom, but any visible display was hidden by the canopy. Carla pushed up near Mannie.

"We have to get out of here, Mannie."

"I'll take your request under advisement," he grumbled.

"If an arrival happens where we're standing—"

"I know that, Carla."

They entered a section of the forest where some of the trees and some of the bushes looked to have grown within one another; sharing the same space.

Carla's resolve hardened. "Mannie."

"I know." He didn't need any encouragement. He knew damn well what could happen. This gorge was a nightmare made real.

The sky darkened and the bizarre world of the forest floor turned incredibly black. There was an explosive splash of color and the hollow boom denoting another arrival. This time, however, the sounds of the arrival were accompanied by a shattering, wood-splitting noise as trees and brush suddenly appeared in the woods beside the group, taking up the same space as the vegetation that was already there, and shards of wood were blasted in all directions.

Everyone in the group dropped to the ground. With the splinters and dust still settling, Devon called out to Mannie. "I'm with Carla," he said in a forced calm. "I think we should get the hell out of here."

"I concur," came the voice of the General from somewhere beyond Devon. "Heartily."

"Well… so long as everyone agrees," said Mannie. He pushed forward, everyone else following right behind. They moved as quickly as the vegetation allowed, which wasn't always as fast as they would have liked. Twice more the sky darkened, followed by the flash of bright, explosive color and the boom of the materialization; both times accompanied by the earsplitting sound of splintering wood.

Mannie stepped out of the forest and into a narrow clearing that ran between the wall of trees and cliff wall rising up from the floor of the gorge. The others came stumbling after him. They spread out, hurrying quickly away from the treeline and as far from the trees as the wall of the gorge allowed.

There was another darkening, another bright crackling of color and then the thunderclap.

Yolanda looked around at the others. *Someone is missing.* "Where's Lee?" she asked.

Each in the group scanned the faces and figures of the others, as if Lee might somehow be hiding in their number. Mannie dropped his pack, spoke with some trepidation.

"Wait here," he said, and started back toward the wall of trees.

In spite of Mannie's suggestion, Carla dropped her own gear and hurried after him. She kept him just within sight. Behind her, several of the group could be seen moving about in clearing.

Mannie stopped. Carla continued forward with a sense of dread. When she reached him, she moved up cautiously beside him.

She saw what he saw.

Part of Lee's head was protruding out of the trunk of a tree. One arm hung limply out of one side.

Yolanda and Ben stood a few yards from the treeline, waiting anxiously for Mannie and Carla to return with news of Lee. Yolanda had an arm around the boy's shoulders.

Robin and Devon sat on a wide, flat stone at the base of the cliff wall, several yards from one another, looking as if they were already certain of the news that Mannie would return with.

The General and the Professor stood well off to one side, speaking quietly amongst themselves.

"The fact that this strip is clear," said the General, "would indicate that we are relatively safe. For the moment."

"We have no idea whether the arrival pattern that we are currently witnessing is normal for this area or is a new phenomenon."

"I agree with your observation, Professor, but not necessarily with the conclusion that you wish to draw from that observation."

"I draw no conclusion. On the contrary, General, it is you wishes to draw suppositions with little or no evidence."

The General calmly placed a hand on the Professor's arm as he looked back in the direction of the others. They watched as Mannie and Carla stepped out of the woods.

Mannie said nothing. Carla looked stricken.

"Oh, dear," the Professor said softly.

Yolanda gripped tightly about Ben's shoulders. Her expression was blank. Ben looked up at her, then wrapped his arms around her waist as if to give her comfort.

Devon lowered his gaze and stared down at the ground between his feet.

Robin stood stiffly, wrapped her arms about herself, as she often did. "He was always off by himself. I don't think we ever said more than a couple of words to one another." She stared down at the rocky ground beneath her feet. "Always busy going about doing something for somebody without being asked. Just did it."

The General cleared his throat. "Good man."

Carla moved over to a dirt mound and dropped down to a sitting position. The Professor walked over and stood beside her, rested a comforting hand on her shoulder.

Mannie stood away from the rest of the group, studied the face of the cliff. He sensed Devon's approach, heard him sigh in a tired way.

"How does it look?" Devon asked.

Mannie only shook his head, took another couple of stumbling steps to one side.

Devon followed, indicated the forest behind them. "I'm not going back in there, Mannie."

"So don't."

"Then don't give me that sad shake of the head." Devon nodded sharply at the cliff. "How does it look?"

"Looks good," said Mannie.

Devon gave an exaggerated nod. "That wasn't so hard, was it?"

Mannie breathed noisily then, looked left along the base of the cliff. A hundred feet further along, the trees grew closer along the wall. He turned his attention again to the cliff directly in front of them.

"We can't go up here," he said. He pointed to the right. "That way is no better."

With that, they both looked again to their left. The forest was thick right up to the base of the cliff. Devon tried to sound optimistic.

"Maybe it's clear again, once we get beyond that stand."

Mannie looked as though he was trying to see through the trees and beyond.

"Maybe. Hope so." He looked then over at the rest of the group.

"Come on," he said, and they walked back to the others. They gathered up their gear as they encouraged everyone to their feet. Within minutes they were traveling along the base of the cliff, a few yards apart, one behind the other.

They stayed close to the cliff, occasionally had to dodge rocks that broke loose from above and rolled down, some splintering as they hit bottom, some crashing noisily into the woods.

Mannie continued looking for a viable way up the cliff, the others willing to follow blindly along, letting him search for the best route up.

It was another hour or more, and getting close to dusk, before Mannie came to a hesitant stop. He stepped back, head back, and studied the rocks and shadows that hovered above them.

At this spot, the treeline was about twenty feet from the cliff. The cliff itself had a much more gradual slope here than what they had been seeing up to this point.

Devon came up beside Mannie. "Not too bad," he said.

Mannie looked at the sky overhead. It was still clear. The cliff wall, however, was in early evening shadow.

"We'd never make it to the top before nightfall."

"I don't want to spend the night down here," said Devon. They had experienced another arrival just a few minutes earlier, and not far inside the trees.

"You'd rather climb a cliff in the dark?"

"Yes," Devon said emphatically. "Yes I would."

Carla came up and stood between them. "Me too," she said.

"That's crazy," said Mannie.

"I don't care," Devon said firmly.

Mannie studied the faces of Devon and Carla as carefully as he had studied the face of the cliff. He looked then at the others, now coming in close.

The General examined the sloping wall towering above them. "An easy climb at the base," he said, "though it is difficult to see what it may be like further up." He turned to Mannie, an apologetic look on his face. "I'll go along with the voice of the majority on this one, Mr. Alvarez. I agree wholeheartedly with your assessment as to the foolishness of starting up at this time of day, but my gut says to get the hell out of here."

Devon gave a sharp nod. "I think his gut speaks for all of us."

"It does," Carla said shortly. "Definitely."

Mannie shook his head sadly, but adjusted his pack with a surrendering shrug of his shoulder and began the climb without comment.

The General spoke up again, directing his words up to Mannie's receding figure.

"If we travel quickly, and if the way is not too terribly formidable, perhaps we could make it to the top before the fading light becomes a danger."

"Whatever," Mannie mumbled without looking down.

Midway up the cliff. Mannie slide-stepped horizontally along a narrow ledge, looking for a way to continue upslope. The sun had set and the evening was gray and beginning to fill with shadows.

Devon was beside Mannie, the General several paces beyond Devon. The others trailed quietly beside and below the General, each two or three paces beyond the other, the line of climbers disappearing around a jut of rock.

Mannie stepped out onto a wide flat ledge, thirty feet deep and sixty feet across. At the back of the ledge, the cliff wall rose straight up to the darkening sky.

Mannie took a few moments to shake out the jitters and then began looking for a possible way up. He could see nothing in the maze of shadows. The top of the cliff was still another hundred yards above them.

Devon stepped up beside him, and the General came up on his other side a moment later. Both dropped their gear at their feet.

Back along the trail, someone set some rocks loose. They heard the sound of stone striking against stone, the gloomy resonance fading into the shadows below, all the way to the floor of the gorge.

The General quietly cleared his throat. "I would not be averse to spending the night right here," he said.

"Nor I," said Devon, choosing not to look directly at Mannie.

Mannie only nodded a silent affirmative, walked slowly toward the back of the ledge and dropped his pack at the foot of the next rise of cliff.

The General turned to the group at large, most of whom had now made it safely onto the ledge. "It is growing much too dangerous to continue," he said authoritatively. "We will be spending the night here and going the rest of the way up in the morning."

"Is that such a good idea?" Robin sounded anxious about spending the night halfway up a cliff.

"We should be safe enough here," said the General.

Devon couldn't let it go at that, and spoke out to no one in particular. "I would suggest that if you are a restless sleeper that you make your bed near the back."

Once settled and as comfortable as they could be in their situation, they ate a light dinner of cold rations and watched the sky finish its transformation to the now familiar alien night; a tapestry of dark blues, purples, and blacks.

There was little conversation, and it wasn't long before, one by one, each set about to get what sleep they could, curling up under the thin blankets they had brought with them.

Mannie woke after only a few hours, and when he was unable to get back to sleep he quietly stepped away from the others and walked out to the lip of the ledge. Sitting on the very edge, legs hanging over the side, he let the scene envelope him.

Overhead was the shell of plum colored night sky. Below him was the canopy of the bizarre forest that covered the floor of the gorge, now in shades of black. And across the gorge, he could see the sheer face that was the far wall. Beyond, spread out beneath the alien sky, stretched the flat plain, shimmering faintly against the glow of the night.

Carla rose up from one of the shadows at the back of the ledge. She approached the edge of the shelf and sat down beside Mannie. At first neither spoke, and when Carla did finally say something, her voice was low, so as not to disturb the others.

"Looks like the arrivals have finally stopped."

Mannie gave a slight nod. "Can't sleep?" he asked.

"Not very well."

"Me neither." Long sigh. "I think I miss my shack."

Again silence. In the long pause, they heard someone snoring peacefully back in the shadows.

"Mannie," Carla said softly, "whatever I may have said, whatever happens, it was the right choice... us leaving town."

Mannie replied with another silent nod.

"I didn't know it then, consciously, but... I never would have left if I hadn't believed, somewhere deep down in this brain of mine, that it was the right thing to do." She gave his arm a soft pat. "You're doing a good job... natural leader."

"I'm not the leader," he grumbled. "I'm not in charge."

Carla grinned. "If you say so."

"I say so."

They again fell silent. Mannie had nothing to say, and Carla struggled with what to say next.

"Would I have liked you back in the real world?" she finally asked.

"I don't know. Do you like me now?"

"Don't know for sure. 'spect so."

"Well," Mannie was starting to grow uncomfortable, "I'm the same now as I was then."

"I doubt that. This place changes people." Carla looked directly at Mannie. "You were a school teacher, right?"

"Third grade."

She took a moment to process that. "You don't seem much like a school teacher to me."

"You're seeing me a bit out of my element."

The comment faded into a long silence in which neither looked at the other. A minute passed before Carla sighed imperceptibly. "I wonder how Mrs. Johansen is doing," she said quietly.

They continued to sit there in the quiet of the night, the strange alien sky overhead, the gorge in shadows below them, the flat plain in the distance beyond the far wall.

Mannie brought his hands up and nudged himself over the top of the cliff, brought his knee up and pushed himself up to his feet.

And he found himself looking at a man sitting on the ground some forty feet away, legs crossed and hands resting in his lap, fingers intertwined.

It was Lucas, the mysterious young man who had observed the group from the shadows back on the plain. He showed no emotion at Mannie's appearance.

Mannie pushed back his surprise and started forward, approaching the stranger. Behind Mannie, Devon climbed up from the gorge, quickly sorted out the scene and followed Mannie.

"Well, well," he said, perhaps to Mannie, perhaps to the stranger.

Mannie stopped three paces from the stranger. Not taking his eyes off the man, he let his pack slide from his shoulders and fall gently to the ground.

"Good morning," he said.

"Good morning," said Lucas, looking calmly up at Mannie.

Mannie glanced behind the stranger, saw only scattered scrub brush, a few trees here and there, and the mountain range, much closer now.

"You live around here?" he asked, turning his attention back to the man.

"Nope." With that, Lucas shifted position and stood up.

"So what are you doing here?" asked Devon.

Lucas smiled and held his hand to Mannie. His physical appearance was non-threatening, but the smooth calmness and the glittering gleam in the eyes were unsettling.

"I've been waiting for you," he said. "The name's Lucas."

Mannie took the hand and shook it. "Mannie Alvarez."

Lucas nodded greeting, then reached a hand out to Devon. Devon gave it a cool study before finally accepting it.

"John Devon," he said.

"Hello," answered Lucas. The others in the group had by now made it off the cliff face and approached. Lucas shook hands with some, gave a friendly nod to others.

Mannie wasn't ready to be friends just yet. "What do you mean, you've been waiting for us?"

Lucas indicated Yolanda. "Specifically, for her."

Yolanda stiffened. "Excuse me?"

"What the hell does that mean?" Mannie asked sharply.

"Sorry," Lucas smiled sheepishly. He struggled for the right words. "I get, well…"

"Well, what?"

"Sorry. I've never had to put it into words before." He gave an apologetic shrug. "Visions, I guess you'd say."

"Huh?" Devon cocked his head to one side.

"What he said," said Mannie.

"Pictures." Lucas fumbled. "Images. In my head. The last few days, I've been getting them from her."

"These pictures, they told you we were coming?" Mannie didn't sound as though he was believing any of this.

"Sort of. Like I said, it's difficult to put into words."

"So it would seem."

"The images that I get from people, from some people, usually have some meaning that I can interpret."

Devon sounded almost as doubtful as Mannie. "And what did these postcards from Yolanda tell you?" he asked.

Lucas gave Devon an uncertain smile. "Pardon?"

Mannie grew increasingly impatient. "Having a great time, wish you were here... yada yada yada. And?"

Lucas lost his smile and spoke matter-of-factly. "You left your town a few weeks ago. I don't know why, but it was important that you leave." He turned his head to look behind him. "You're going to the mountains."

"Yeah." Mannie was hesitant.

"If it's all right with you, I'd like to go with you."

Mannie didn't look particularly surprised at this. He glanced over at Devon, who shrugged noncommittally. Mannie then looked back over his shoulder. The General was frowning.

The Professor appeared more accepting. "We were all strangers at one time," he said.

The General grunted loudly in the general direction of the stranger.

"What information can you provide regarding our destination, sir?"

The Professor tried to soften the tone. "Are you hungry?" he asked. "We don't have much, I'm afraid, but what little there is, we will share."

Lucas spoke up before anyone else could chime in. "That's very kind of you." He reached into his coat pocket and pulled out a small apple. He tossed it to Devon.

Devon grabbed it out of the air, studied, smelled it. He held it out for the others to see, finally tossed it to young Ben.

Lucas nodded at Ben and the apple. "I can take you to more of those," he said.

It wasn't the prettiest apple that Devon had ever seen, but...

"Lead on, my man," he said.

They travelled through grassy, gently rolling foothills. Scrub brush was now more common, as was short, twisted oak and alder.

Rising above them, yet still some distance away, were the taller, more rugged mountains.

Lucas led the way. Mannie and Yolanda walked beside him, the others following along behind, forming a straggling line fifty yards long.

Lucas answered a question from Yolanda. "No, it isn't a matter of reading your thoughts or your mind," he said. "I'm not getting into your brain. I only receive what you project out."

"I'm sending out images?"

"I believe Mr. Devon called them postcards." The word 'postcards' sounded foreign coming from Lucas.

"I had no idea," said Yolanda. "I mean, my grandmother was said to have visions and the like, but I never. Do you send out... postcards?"

"I don't think so. But then, I really don't know. I've never met another receiver, like me. So, who knows?"

"Then I might receive as well as send," said Yolanda, wondering.

"Perhaps we can find out?"

They group wandered down into a wild, overgrown apple orchard. The trees were misshapen from years of unmanaged growth. The apples were small and discolored.

Robin pulled one from a low branch and bit into it.

"Not too bad," she said through a mouthful of apple. She quickly finished it off, tossed the core aside, and picked another. The others began pulling fruit from the lower branches.

Twenty minutes later, everyone was scattered about the orchard, most sitting, paired off and talking quietly.

Mannie sat alone with his back against the trunk of one of the apple trees. His eyes were closed, but he opened them when heard someone approaching.

Devon eased himself down. "Lucas says that we should head for a valley not too far off, not too high in the mountains."

"Why," asked Mannie.

"Food, water."

Mannie leaned forward a little and looked in the direction of Lucas, who was sitting with Yolanda. The two of them appeared to be in pleasant conversation.

Mannie furrowed his brow. "If there's a nice little valley in the mountains with food and water, and Lucas knows about it, then what is he doing out here?"

"Couldn't tell ya', Mannie. You think he's up to something?"

"Of course he's up to something."

"That doesn't mean he doesn't have our best interests at heart."

Mannie was not amused. "No doubt." He gave a long, serious look across the orchard at Lucas. "He's a strange one, and I'm not talking about that weird connection he has with Yolanda."

"But that is peculiar."

"Yeah, but… he has… a familiarity… with this place."

"Maybe he's been around here a lot longer than the rest of us."

Mannie slowly shook his head.

He's way too comfortable here… thought Mannie. He slowly shook his head. "It's not just that. This comes from… knowledge."

Mannie continued to watch Lucas and Yolanda. Lucas seemed to sense that he was being observed. He looked in Mannie's direction. He gave a friendly nod, completely innocent, then returned to his conversation with his new friend.

Chapter Three

From a distance, the waterfall was a thin ribbon of silver slicing through a growth of dark green covering a steep mountainside, threading down to a misty pool at the base. The top of the fall looked to be borne from the sky.

The group hiked and climbed a rugged path that wound its way up the slope, following close to one side of the waterfall. They climbed in silence, the roar of the waterfall a constant backdrop suppressing any other sounds.

As they climbed up over the lip of the waterfall, an alien landscape stretched out before them; a wide valley with rolling hills bordering either side that spread away, reaching out into the distance. The floor of the valley was a grassland with a meandering river in the center that fed the waterfall. A fog-like mist hung low above the river, spread to either side over small meadows. Unfamiliar species of trees clustered together in small groves.

The sky directly overhead was steel blue, a low dome hovering over the valley. As the setting receded toward the far end of the valley, the color shifted to shades of purple, then of deep red.

A large structure sat on a towering rise at the far end of the valley, its tall walls gleaming white against the daylight.

Lucas stepped out ahead of the others, striking out down the center of the valley.

Mannie didn't look happy. After a few moments to take it all in, he started determinedly forward, marching after Lucas.

Devon put on a light, mocking grimace and leaned nearer the General.

"Lucas is in trouble," he snickered.

Lucas reached a slight rise and stopped, stared in the direction of the structure at the far end of the valley. Mannie came up beside him, glanced sharply at the scene set out before them and then turned to face the odd little man.

"What the hell's going on?"

Lucas continued looking at the structure that dominated the end of the valley. "A beautiful sight, isn't it?"

"Lovely," Mannie said impatiently. "What is it?"

Lucas smiled, but there was a hint of uncertainty in the expression.

"Home?" he offered, self–questioning.

"You're not sure?"

Lucas was so long in responding that Mannie didn't think he was going to answer.

"I have been away for a very long time," he said finally.

"But you live here? *Lived* here?"

The General and Devon came up beside Mannie and Lucas.

"I think you owe us an explanation, Lucas," said the General.

Lucas now finally did look away from the scene, looked directly at the General. "Why?" he asked.

"Sir." The General was momentarily taken aback, but quickly regained his composure. "You came to us. You asked to join us, and we welcomed you. You then guided us to this location, suggesting only as to the presence of food and water, while knowing full well what we would in fact find. Now, sir. What is this place, what is that structure, what is your relationship to it—" The General paused a moment, but the others knew that he was not quite finished. "—and why did you think it necessary to seek us out and bring us here?"

Lucas had listened patiently, his smile very faint. Once the General had finished, the smile broadened, just a little, and Lucas rolled his head back and looked to the sky, then the valley, and then the gleaming walls of the structure in the distance. He spread his hands out and took it all in.

"This place. This place is my world," he said. "This valley, the gorge that you passed through, the plain that you crossed over, the town in which you lived. My world." He let his head roll back around to look again at the General, then at the group that had gathered around them. "You are guests here."

Devon leaned forward, looked pointedly at Lucas. "That, my man, would imply that we can leave."

Lucas slowly, with an air of quiet assurance, turned away from the group and looked again in the direction of the distant structure.

"That might be possible, Mr. Devon."

Most were gathered now around a small campfire, the glow reflecting off those sitting nearest it. They had set up camp for the night near the river. The dusk overhead was a wash of dark blues and purples, and there was a bright shimmer to it that shone down on the valley floor.

Lucas sat on the nearby rise, looking out over the valley and the structure in the distance, his silhouette visible against the strange sky.

Mannie stood some distance from Lucas, some distance from the camp. Devon approached him, coming from a brief conversation with Lucas. He gave a faint shrug.

"He grew up here; in this valley, in that castle, or whatever it is. According to him, there's some kind of a *confrontation* looming."

"What is it with him?" asked Mannie. "What's with all the mystery?"

"I don't know."

"What does he want us for?"

"Don't know."

Mannie frowned, looked back at the group gathered around the campfire. While most of the others were looking into the flames of the small fire, Yolanda was looking at Lucas.

Mannie eyed the woman. "She might be able to get more out of him than you did."

"You think she can do what he can do?" asked Devon. "Remember, he doesn't read minds, he only picks up what she sends out."

"Even if that's true, and I'm not saying that it is, how do we know that he isn't sending out too? Sending out exactly what we want to know?"

Devon looked from Yolanda to Lucas, back to Yolanda. He held out a hand then in a silent '*after you*', and followed

Mannie as he started to camp. They settled in beside Yolanda, sitting on either side of her. She gave a knowing nod and smiled somberly.

"You would like to know what Lucas is up to," she stated.

"Hey, she's pretty good," Devon said snidely.

Mannie ignored the sarcasm. "Yes. We would like to know what Lucas is up to; and what he wants with us."

Yolanda slowly shook her head. "He's blocking me."

"You've tried, then?" asked Devon.

"Of course I've tried." Yolanda glanced in Lucas' direction. "And he knows it."

Mannie was also looking at Lucas. "He must have known from the start that you had the ability to pick up images as well as send them."

"How can he be blocking you?" Devon asked. "I thought he could only pick up what you sent out. Wouldn't it be the same in reverse?"

"I don't know. I mean, I think it's just as he said, but I can see that he's putting up something, and it's preventing me from seeing what's there."

As they watched, Lucas turned his head and looked at the three of them. A calm had settled over him.

Yolanda sounded lost, almost frightened. "Listen you guys. This is all brand new to me. I just tell fortunes. I tell tourists what I think they wanna hear. This? This stuff is weird."

"Maybe this place turned on some latent powers you didn't know you had," suggested Devon.

"Or maybe he did," said Mannie. He spoke without turning away from the man's gaze. "I'm not going to blindly follow this guy."

"I agree," said Devon. "Although, I must admit… this valley? Not too bad."

"Maybe."

"What maybe?"

"I don't know." Mannie looked out into the increasing darkness, then up at the sky. "I half expect a dragon to suddenly swoop down breathing fire."

Now it was Devon's turn to look anxiously upward.

Damn it, I hate when he does that…

Mannie was asleep near the dead embers of the campfire. The predawn morning was very quiet. Lucas knelt down and rested a hand on Mannie's shoulder. When he opened his eyes, Mannie somehow managed to not look surprised.

"You need something?" he asked, looking calmly up at the face hovering over him.

"Can we talk?" Lucas asked in answer.

With that, Mannie slowly sat up and swung himself around. He saw that everyone else was still asleep, forming a circle of blanketed bodies a few yards out from the dead campfire. He pushed himself to his feet and followed Lucas out beyond the perimeter of the camp, pulling on his jacket as he walked.

Lucas watched him approach, but said nothing once the two were standing side by side. Mannie stuffed his hands into his pockets.

"What can I do for you, Lucas?" he asked. He tried to look and sound casual, kept his eyes on the scene before them and not this strange man.

Lucas took another moment, breathed in their surroundings.

"Strange world this is, huh?" he asked finally.

"You could say that."

"Anyway, it's what I've heard. I wouldn't know."

Mannie said nothing. There was nothing to say.

Lucas pushed ahead with his thought. "I was brought here when I was a baby." He indicated the large structure in the distance. "I lived there most of my life."

Something about that statement struck Mannie as wrong. It took a moment for him to realize what that was. "But these mountains... they just showed up a few months ago."

"That's right."

"So how can you have spent your life here?"

"Interesting, huh?" Lucas' smirk said *'now you're starting to get it'*.

Mannie was really not happy. He wasn't getting it. He wasn't getting it at all.

"What do you want from us, Lucas? We're not going any further without some answers."

Lucas put on the same 'this is my world' look that he had the day before. He took a step in the direction of the structure. "My brother is in there," he said. "No doubt watching us."

"All right. I take it you and he had a falling out."

"Karl left me here. Alone."

"And?" *What does any of this have to do with us?*

"He's reshaping the world into something of his own making."

"Is that what the *arrivals* are all about? These materializations?"

"He is creating tears in the fabric of space, using pieces of parallel universes to build his own little empire here in this world."

"Your disagreement… it wouldn't have anything to do with who is going to run this empire, would it?"

"I like this world just the way it is." Now it was Lucas who sounded frustrated. "If I can't stop him, my brother will destroy it. And just where do you think that would leave you and your friends, Mr. Alvarez?"

Lucas was leading the way up the center of the valley, Mannie walking beside him. The others trailed along well behind them.

As Devon had said, this wasn't such a bad place. The valley floor green meadows, small groves of trees and the ever-present meandering river. It was all very different than what they had become accustomed to, living out on the plains.

Carla came up beside him. "I thought we weren't going to follow this guy anymore," she said. "Not without some answers."

"He made a compelling argument," said Devon. He wasn't looking at her, wasn't looking at the two walking ahead of him. "You got someplace else you gotta be?"

"This doesn't feel right."

Devon didn't respond, but now Carla had ruined the mood. His expression changed subtly, not that she noticed.

"There's something really wrong here," she went on. "And it's getting more wrong by the minute."

Devon again said nothing, at least not at first. When he finally did speak, his voice was low and he still couldn't bring himself to look at her.

"Yeah," he sighed. *Damn it…*

They continued in silence for another hour before stopping for a break. Lucas wanted to keep going… no reason to stop… *come on, let's go…* but Mannie insisted. He wasn't about to let Lucas run everything.

They stopped again at midday and had a cold lunch. Lucas' impatience drove everyone crazy and they started out again after only a few minutes.

Mid-afternoon. They passed a children's playground, the kind that one might see in a small neighborhood park. There was a swing set, a small merry-go-round, teeter-totter, jungle gym, bars.

Set into the hillside high above the playground loomed the gleaming white castle.

Lucas was giddy with excitement.

Lucas stepped through the great double doors and into the main hall of the castle, Mannie immediately behind him. The room was large, with a high ceiling that allowed a mezzanine at the top of the staircase directly opposite the main doors. The walls and ceiling were bright white. The furniture consisted entirely of a handful of small tables set against the walls.

Lucas rushed toward the stairs as the others came up behind Mannie.

"No place like home, eh?" said Devon.

Mannie didn't answer.

Robin shook her head slowly, speaking barely above a whisper. "I don't much like it."

Lucas ran back and forth along the mezzanine, calling out for his brother, disappearing now and then as he searched the rooms.

"Karl! Come out, come out!" He disappeared then from view and the room grew quiet.

Mannie lowered his gaze and looked around at the others in the group. Some began moving away from the front door and were cautiously exploring. They looked through the occasional door, though for the moment no one left the main hall.

"What do you think, Mannie?" asked Devon. "Nobody home?"

Mannie gave a noncommittal shrug. Lucas reappeared at the top of the staircase, paused a moment, then half bounced as he stomped down the stairs. He turned quickly and hurried to his left, disappeared through another set of double-doors.

Mannie was watching the doors, waiting for Lucas' return, when a movement drew his attention back to the mezzanine.

Karl stood stoically at the top of the staircase. His imposing figure was in stark contrast to that of his brother Lucas. He had an air about him that defined him as the master of the house.

He watched silently as everyone worked their way back to the center of the main hall. Once all were gathered together, Mannie took several steps forward.

Karl appeared to inspect each member of the group before finally speaking.

"Welcome," he stated coolly. The single word denoted nothing in the way of Karl's feeling at this invasion of his home.

"Thank you," said Mannie. "You must be Karl."

Karl took two steps downs the stairs, slow and confident. His presence dominated the room.

"You must be friends of my brother," he said.

"Friend might be too strong a word," said Mannie.

Karl smiled knowingly. "I understand completely."

Midway down the staircase, Karl stopped and watched Lucas come back into the main hall. When he spoke to his brother, it was both friendly and ominous.

"Lucas, my boy. So good to see you."

Lucas paused, then took another two steps. His physical presence changed, his self-confidence draining. He tried to get it back, struggled within himself and fought to put on the face of confidence.

"Karl... kind of you to make an appearance."

"Oh, Lucas. Actually, I've been waiting for you. So looking forward to getting together, reminiscing over old times." Karl took another step down the staircase. "How has the world been treating you? You look well."

"It could have been worse."

"I'm so glad." Karl turned then to look at the group as a whole. "Refreshments?"

With that he descended the stairs and walked casually to the set of doors opposite those that Lucas had taken. He expected the others to follow.

The room they entered was glass-domed, the ceiling a hemisphere of metal ribs and thick plates of glass that reached down nearly to the floor. The alien sky was visible overhead; the valley below stretched out to the horizon.

The floor of the observatory was concrete, with cobblestone pathways wandering in and around tables, benches, and several telescopes on tripods. Plants grew in raised beds that lined the paths.

Karl stepped behind a serving table. On the table were several glass pitchers, a number of glasses, and a tray of cookies and breads.

Karl lifted a pitcher and began filling glasses.

"I find this particular juice to be very refreshing," he said. "I trust that you will as well."

Mannie was wary, but the Professor moved in and picked up a glass. He took a cautious sip, nodded appreciatively. Several others then moved forward and reached for glasses of juice and cookies.

The Professor indicated the spread of drink and snacks. "You were expecting us," he said.

Karl silently indicated the scene outside, with the view of the valley floor and the path they had taken to reach the castle.

"Of course," said the Professor.

Devon washed down a mouthful of cookie with a big swallow of juice. "Helluva a layout you have here," he managed to say.

"My father was quite the architect," said Karl. "This observatory… this was for my mother."

Karl glanced over at Lucas then and there was a very uncomfortable moment. The look from Karl was one of disappointment; the look from Lucas was one of suppressed anger, but also of apprehension.

"You live here all alone, now?" asked the General.

Karl again looked at Lucas, this time more sharply, before responding to the General.

"That's right," he said unemotionally.

"If I might ask, sir, how is it that you are here? I have the impression that you did not arrive in the same manner as the rest of us."

"That is correct. Our father brought us." Karl smiled at Lucas. "Is that not right, dear boy?"

"I wouldn't know," stated Lucas.

"Of course you do." Karl turned to the entire group. "But then, Lucas was quite young when Father created this world."

This last statement took everyone by surprise. Devon was the first to speak up.

"What's that?"

"And Lucas and our father never did get along," continued Karl. He lifted a brow and eyed Lucas. "Would you not agree?"

"Got along well enough."

Devon tried to interject, looking for an answer to his question. "Excuse me. About this whole *creating the world* thing…"

"Yes. Quite," adds the General.

Karl feigned genuine surprise. "Are you saying that Lucas never mentioned it?"

"Not in so many words, no," said Devon.

"Not in any words," the General stated.

"I see," said Karl. "Yes. I can understand why he might not want to broach the subject of our father." He again looked over at Lucas. There was clearly something unspoken going on between them.

Lucas, for his part, had managed to regain at least some of his self-assurance, but his negative emotions were making it difficult for him to maintain a clear head.

Karl took a long drink, then held the glass out before him and looked at it appreciatively.

"This world did exist in some fashion, of course," he said. "This alternate plane was here. What my father did, what our father did, was to bring together the elements necessary to construct this physical reality that you see now all around you."

The Professor was dumbfounded. "Absolutely amazing," he managed to get out.

"Or absolutely insane," said Carla.

"Father is a genius, my dear," said Karl, smiling softly. "Intensely brilliant. But I grant you that he is quite… eccentric."

Carla fell silent under Karl's glittering gaze, the man's smile taking on a painted look.

The General spoke up. "But why on earth would anyone do such a thing?"

"Come now, General…" the Professor interjected. "The man created a world."

"And look what he did with it." The General was not as awestruck by the achievement as the Professor. "We were kidnapped, literally wrenched from our lives, and brought here to squalid lives of meager existence, barely able to survive at all."

Karl stiffened and his face grew dark. "That, sir, was not my father's doing."

"Of course it was," Lucas jumped in. "His and yours."

Karl looked studiously at Lucas, finally gave a subtle nod. "Lucas, Lucas… what <u>do</u> you have in mind? Do you think to somehow remove *me* as well?"

Mannie, who had been standing near the glass wall, moved nearer to Karl and the rest of the group. "What happened to your parents, Karl?" he asked.

"Ah. A very important question. The answer to which unravels the mystery."

"He killed them," said Lucas, spitting out the words.

"I don't think so," Mannie said calmly.

"Very perceptive, sir," said Karl.

Carla looked from Karl to Lucas and back again. "Lucas killed them?" she asked.

"They live yet," said Karl. "At least, I believe they do."

"What happened to them?"

Karl looked carefully at the drink in his hand, set it down and looked sadly at Lucas. After several moments, he turned back to Carla.

"There are an incalculable number of unfinished worlds, like this one, each existing in an alternate plane, empty but for these barren wastelands of planets." He nodded in the direction of Lucas. "My brother sent our parents to one of these."

Mannie took another step nearer Karl. He wasn't about to be drawn into an emotional tug-of-war. He spoke quickly to his own line of thought.

"When?" he asked.

"Some time before the first of you would have arrived."

"That's a lie!" Lucas said sharply.

"I don't think so." Mannie remained calm.

"I went looking for them," said Karl.

"And you took this castle with you," said Mannie.

"And this valley. And these mountains."

The Professor understood. "So that they would be able to see you, even if you were not able to see them."

"Yes."

"And now you're back," Devon piped in, "and the mountains are back."

"You weren't able to find your parents?" asked Carla, though it was more of an observation than a question.

"No. I am afraid not."

Mannie, Devon and Yolanda stood near the glass wall that looked out across the valley. The others were scattered about the observatory in small groups.

Mannie looked across the room at Karl and Lucas. The two were in a heated discussion. Lucas looked angry, while Karl was apparently trying to keep things civil. He lifted a hand and rested it on the smaller man's shoulder. Lucas shoved it aside.

Devon let out a questioning sigh. "Waddya think, Mannie?"

"I'll believe Karl before I'll believe Lucas, but I wouldn't trust either one."

"You seemed to connect with big brother."

"What he had to say made sense, but that doesn't mean he's not keeping something from us; something that could hurt us."

"There was truth in his words," said Yolanda. "I could sense it."

Devon grinned. "You mean that weird connection of yours?"

"Simple intuition."

"Not... uh..."

Yolanda only shrugged, and Devon nodded thoughtfully and looked back at the brothers on the other side of the observatory.

"Well, if he is telling the truth," Devon went on, "and he's not asking anything of us, I'm going to have to side with Karl."

"He's telling a truth, not necessarily the truth."

"Don't start slicing words on me, Yolanda," said Devon.

"Who says he's not asking anything of us?" asked Mannie. "Give him time."

"Will you two give me a break?" groaned Devon. "I don't even know what we're doing here."

Mannie lowered his gaze and gave Devon a somber look. "Lucas asked for our help." It may have been an accusation, but was more likely a simple observation.

Before Devon could come up with a witty retort, the General stepped into the conversation. "Which he has yet to call us on. In what manner was this assistance to take?"

Devon jabbed a thumb in Yolanda's general direction. "Something she was supposed to do."

"I don't think he's ready." Yolanda looked curiously in the direction of Karl and Lucas. "Whatever he was expecting here, he got something different."

"Well, you keep your mind in access mode, or whatever it is," said Devon. "And listen out for what either one is up to."

With that, the four grew quiet. They could just hear the harsh tones coming from the heated discussion continuing across the room, but couldn't quite make out the words.

Mannie turned and looked out at the darkening sky. When he spoke, it was little more than a mumble.

"I'm thinking there might yet be a dragon coming out of the sky, breathing fire and vengeance down on all of us."

It took everything that Devon had not to turn and look out at that same sky.

Damn it, enough with the dragon crap, already...

The hallway was wide and lined with dark, heavy doors. Several brass lamps hanging on pale walls provided an iridescent glow.

Karl had already shown most of the others to their rooms. Behind him, Carla was just disappearing through the door beyond Karl and Mannie.

Karl opened the next door.

"And this would be yours, Mr. Alvarez," he said.

Mannie stepped past Karl and started into the room. "Thank you."

"My pleasure. Sleep well."

Doubt that, thought Mannie. He heard the door close behind him.

The room was clean, almost antiseptic. There was a single bed, a chair, and one table. Drawers were built into one wall, beside a sliding panel.

Mannie moved toward the panel, pulled it aside. As he did, a light within the compartment came on. It was an empty closet.

He slid the panel closed and stepped away, moved toward a glass door in the far wall. He came out onto a private balcony, moved to the railing and rested his forearms on the top bar, leaned forward and admired the scene before him.

The night sky was a very dark blue, with no stars; but there was a glow to it that illuminated the valley that was splayed out before him. The river meandering down its center had a flickering luminosity, the hills to either side of the valley were hovering, dark silhouettes.

Carla stepped out on the balcony beside Mannie's. They acknowledged one another, but neither broke the eerie silence that seemed to lay heavily over them.

At the center of the wide, flat roof was a workstation surrounded by an encircling, three-foot high glass-walled perimeter. Above the roof, above the workstation, was the same great shell of night sky that Mannie and Carla were admiring.

Lucas stood within the workstation. He glanced only briefly at the approaching figure of his brother Karl. He casually flipped one switch, then another. Nothing happened.

Karl didn't appear to be overly concerned with Lucas' actions. He walked into the workstation area, glanced at one panel, then another, not really interested in what he was seeing. He pulled a tall stool toward him and slid onto it.

"What are you after, Lucas? What do you want?"

Lucas flipped another switch, flipped it back, without looking at his brother.

"You stole my home from me, Karl," he said.

"You stole my family from me, dear brother."

"Yeah, well…" Lucas smiled modestly. "We could have accomplished a lot together. The world we could have built."

"We don't want the same world," Karl said tiredly. "I intend to make things right. I am going to rectify the damage that you have done."

"Return this world to that empty existence we had before? I don't think so." Lucas absently flipped the switch back and forth, again and again. Nothing happened, but then he didn't expect it to.

"Think as you wish, brother."

"There is much left to do." He indicated the workstation around them. "I can now continue my work."

Karl tapped at his temple. "Not without the key."

"Yes. I know." Lucas grinned. "Your *integration* into the system."

"It won't work without recognition."

"I have not forgotten," said Lucas, fully confident now. "It was a nice upgrade. You had me for a while."

Karl chose to say nothing. *Let the boy hang himself.*

Lucas' grin broadened to a full smile. Now he tapped at his temple. "I am not without resources… *dear brother.*"

Karl shook his head sadly. "There is no other way in, Lucas."

Lucas could see Yolanda in his mind, sharp and clear. She was in her room. She was asleep.

"I know," he said. "Your key will do."

Yolanda's eyes fluttered opened. *Fear…*

"That will never happen," said Karl.

"It already has."

Yolanda was unable to move. Panic… *oh my god…*

Lucas was in control. "A simple matter, really."

He flipped a switch.

Karl could see it, could feel it.

"Lucas. No."

The world around them exploded in a tremendous shattering of color. In a flash then, all color beyond the rooftop washed to black.

Everything around them vanished.

Mannie stepped cautiously out onto his balcony. The scene was surreal. The castle they were in was now suspended in a black void. Scattered out in the distance were fragments of landscape hovering in the black.

Several cracks of lightening sent blazes of bright blue across the surface of the fragments before the shadows washed back over them.

Carla stepped out onto her own balcony. She moved slowly to the railing.

"What is this place?"

Mannie shook his head uncertainly. *How the hell would I know?*

"What happened?" Carla asked, as much to the void around them as to Mannie.

This time, Mannie had an answer. "The dragon…"

Lucas took a step back from Karl, kept himself just out of the reach of his brother.

Karl took a step closer. "Take us back," he said sharply.

"Oh, I have no intention of staying here," said Lucas.

"Don't play games, boy."

Lucas lost all sense of joviality. He was now quite serious in tone and manner.

"No games," he said. "I'm going back. You are not."

"Don't do this." Karl spoke firmly. He would not show doubt or fear.

"The woman has your mind imprint," said Lucas. "I have our father's toys. I have my home."

"Lucas…"

"What more? Time to go." Lucas felt something akin to joy. "I have a world to build."

Karl took another step nearer. This time, Lucas didn't step back. He glanced at the work panel, which was now midway between the two of them.

Karl smiled menacingly. "I think we have a point of contention that needs sorting out, don't you? Dear brother?"

Lucas didn't look as confident as he did just a moment earlier. The dominating air of big brother pushed threateningly at him.

Damn him.

His gaze shifted quickly from the panel and back to Karl. He started to think that he might just lose control of the situation.

Damn him, damn him…

Karl let the menacing look fade, leaving a coldly dead calm. "Did you really believe that you could just walk in and take all this away from me? I am not as weak, nor as naïve, as our father, dear boy."

He lifted his hand several inches, held it out so that it hovered near the panel. A visible spark jumped from his fingers down to the Plexiglas. Several small indicator lights flickered.

Lucas realized what was about to happen. He jumped at the panel and slapped at the controls.

"No!"

He wasn't in time, not that he could have done anything about it. Blue lightning cracked overhead, spidering across the great shell that enclosed the world, bathing the rooftop in the bright, blue glow.

Karl and Lucas were seized in a fractured moment in time.

The fragments of worlds hanging like ornaments in the black void rushed in on the vortex of the lonely white castle.

Yolanda was unable to move, was uncertain even that she still existed. Her terror was visible only in the glimmer of her eyes.

Lucas screamed out in anger and pain. Karl's face stiffened in fierce determination. The universe around them filled with the rush of fragments of worlds coming from a thousand different realities.

Mannie and Carla stood as silent observers on the tiny balconies, awash in the blue glow of the flashing of the blue lightning. Shadows drifted across their silhouettes as world fragments rushed toward them and past them.

All grew suddenly very slow and deathly quiet. The inrush of small worldlets toward the castle, the center of this bizarre fulcrum, gradually slowed to a near stop.

Carla turned her head in slow motion and stared at Mannie.

Mannie sensed that she was looking at him, slowly turned from the magnificent scene in front of them and looked at Carla.

Neither knew what to say, what words to speak to break the enchantment they found themselves at the heart of.

Yolanda, alone in her room, felt the paralysis ease. The muscles throughout her body, the taut lines across her face relaxed. She let her head roll slowly to one side…

She stood in the middle of an open plain. She turned her head slowly, completing the movement begun a moment before.

She turned her body; slowly, very slowly…

So many different views from so many different worlds. Each line of sight revealed a different sky, a different horizon.

In some worlds there were people. In most worlds there were not.

All the worlds… all at once.

Yolanda stopped.

Something was wrong… something was very wrong…

Please no…

Not Yolanda.

Lucas…

Lucas stood two paces from Karl.

Shock, surprise… horror shown on Lucas' face.

Karl spoke softly, but there was no remorse.

"Sorry, boy."

Alone in her room, Yolanda screamed out in agony.

Taking a shuffling step back from the balcony railing, Mannie watched the sky before him shatter into millions of tiny pieces, each a glittering blue.

A moment later the universe turned completely black.

On the rooftop, Lucas collapsed forward. Karl stepped up quickly and took hold of him, eased his brother to the floor. He stood then and moved into position before the work console. He held his hand over the panel. Again a spark jumped from his fingers.

Mannie watched as the black void beyond the balcony dissolved to the scene of the valley.

Everything looked exactly as it had earlier.

"That's some dragon," said Carla. Her hands held tight to the railing of her balcony.

Mannie started to grin, but realization swept over his face. He turned about and hurried from the balcony.

Coming into the hallway, he saw the Professor enter Yolanda's room, the General right him. The room was crowded by the time Mannie got there. He found himself standing inside the door.

Robin was sitting on the bed beside Yolanda. When she glanced up at Mannie, she looked lost.

Carla came in, pushed her way through and approached the bed. "What's going on?" she asked, not to anyone in particular.

"I think she's in a coma," said Robin.

"But how?"

"If I had to guess," said Devon, standing with his back against the wall, "I'd say that Lucas has done whatever it was he was planning; whatever he needed her for."

Mannie didn't need to see anymore. He turned about and left the room. Devon followed him several seconds later.

Carla continued looking down at Yolanda. "What could have happened?"

The Professor spoke for the first time. "I have no doubt that Mr. Devon is correct. That Lucas fellow used Miss Yates to nefarious purposes, most likely to overcome the power of his brother." He looked anxiously at the door, then at the General. "Perhaps we should follow Mannie."

At that moment, Ben came into room.

"You two go ahead," said Carla. "We'll catch up."

Mannie came into the main hall from a side door, Devon right behind him, just as the Professor and the General started down the staircase from the mezzanine.

"No sign of them?" asked the Professor.

"It's a big building," said Devon.

The four of them met at the foot of the stairs. The General looked about them, his expression dark and his tone of voice darker.

"Perhaps we should call out in some manner," he stated. "Alert our host to our desire for a dialog."

Karl appeared at the top of the stairs. "That will not be necessary, gentlemen." He looked then to his right as Carla came out onto the mezzanine, Robin

and young Ben right behind her. Karl
accompanied them downstairs. Once
gathered together, he made a quick
visual sweep of the group.

"I apologize if the disagreement
between my brother and myself alarmed
anyone," he said.

"It did much more than that, sir," said
the General.

"Something's happened to Yolanda,"
said Robin.

Karl looked genuinely surprised,
though not particularly upset. "That is
unfortunate."

"That's it?" Carla spouted, an
accusation more than a question.

"What would you have me do,
Madam?"

"What was all that?" asked Mannie.
"What happened?"

Carla wasn't finished yet. "What
happened to Yolanda?"

Karl studied both Mannie and Carla,
as if trying to decide which question to

respond to. He let out a thoughtful, if calculated, sigh.

"My brother attempted to wrest control of… *of this*… from me." He indicated the world around them. "He used your friend as a conduit to gain access to the system. Connected the way they were, it would seem that Lucas brought her down with him."

"Then your brother—" Devon started.

"What was it we saw?" Mannie cut him off.

"All the worlds, all at once," said Karl. He turned an eye to Devon. "My brother is dead, Mr. Devon."

Chapter Four

Most of the group had gathered in the conservatory, all but Carla and Robin, who sat with Yolanda in her room. Mannie stood at the glass wall, looking out at the valley. The sky outside was splashed with this world's idea of evening colors. He could hear the Professor and the General, sitting together on a nearby bench, arguing in hushed voices.

Devon came up beside Mannie, looked through the glass and saw the same valley that Mannie saw. "What do we do now?" he asked.

"I don't have the slightest idea," said Mannie.

"We can't stay here."

"I'm open to suggestions." Mannie looked side-glance at Devon.

"That dude whacked his brother, and I don't think he minded doing it," said Devon. "He's as batty as Lucas ever was."

"At the moment, we have nowhere to go; and I'm not leaving Yolanda behind."

Devon grimaced at that. "Carla says she's the same."

Mannie had already heard the same. He looked over at the General and the Professor. They had stopped their discussion and were looking over in Mannie's direction. He glanced back at the one and only door. He looked hard at Devon.

"We need her," he said. "She may be our only way home."

Mannie stepped out onto the rooftop and started across toward the workstation enclosure. Karl stood in its heart, moving calmly from panel to panel. He acknowledged Mannie's arrival without stopping what he was doing or even looking up from his work.

"Good evening, sir."

"Karl," Mannie said calmly.

"You have questions, Mr. Alvarez."

"A few."

Karl continued his work. "Concerns," he stated.

"A few."

Karl lifted his attention from one of the panels and looked at Mannie for the first time.

"You are hoping to return home… you and your friends," he said. "I am guessing that Lucas promised this in return for your assistance."

"Something like that."

"With Lucas no longer among us, you are afraid that your way out has been closed to you."

"If such a way ever actually existed."

Karl's grin was unsettling. "The key question. The answer to which all else rests."

"And whether or not you will help us."

Karl dropped his gaze from Mannie down to the panels of the workstation. He spoke as he returned to his work.

"If such a thing were possible, what manner of host would I be to deny your request for assistance? Unfortunately, it is not possible. I cannot return you to your world. I am sorry."

With that, Karl flipped a switch, straightened and backed away from the panel. He stepped out of the workstation and walked several paces. He stopped then and looked out to the horizon.

There was no sound, but there was a visible burst of color and light far in the distance.

Karl spoke over his shoulder. "It will take much for me to repair the damage done by my brother," he said.

Mannie looked from the horizon back to Karl.

"But you had this equipment with you all this time," he said. "How could he have caused all this?"

"In addition to stranding our parents on some half-formed world, Lucas managed to set a number of things in motion before I was able to stop him. Most of what you see beyond the valley was created, and is still forming, from the seeds that he planted years ago."

Karl turned about and returned to the workstation. Stepping inside, he again hovered over the panels. "I must locate each of these seeds and undo what they have borne."

"Then why can't you undo our being brought here?" asked Mannie. "Send us back?"

Karl spoke in short, curt words. "Because I don't know where you come from."

Mannie was startled. He stiffened, lifted a hand and pointed in the direction of the horizon they had been looking at a minute earlier.

"Then what are you doing with all that?"

"I am removing from my world that which does not belong."

The General and Devon stood just inside the door of Mannie's room, watched Mannie come out of the bathroom wiping a wet cloth across his face.

Devon looked frustrated. "What the hell did he mean by that?" he asked Mannie.

"He thinks Lucas fouled up the pristine world that their father created, and he plans on setting it right."

"So send us home."

"He says he doesn't know how."

"And you think he's telling the truth?"

"I don't know."

The General was frowning. "Do you think Lucas really knew? How to send us back?"

"I don't know that either," said Mannie.

"If there is a way," said the General, "we need to find it."

Devon let out a dark, tired sigh. "Right now, that needs to be second on our 'To Do' list."

"Yeah," sighed Mannie.

"I suppose you're right," said the General.

"Of course I'm right. I'm not going to be *removed* without a fight."

At that moment there was a knock at the door and the Professor stuck his head in.

"Yolanda is awake."

Mannie was the last to make his way into Yolanda's crowded room. He pushed his way through the others and stood beside the bed. Robin was sitting beside Yolanda, who looked up at Mannie.

"Waddya say, Yolanda?"

"I say hey."

"How are you feeling?"

"Not too bad."

Mannie looked for a spot and sat down on the bed next to Robin.

"Did they tell you what happened?"

Yolanda took his hand. "They told me."

"Do you remember much of it?"

Yolanda looked carefully at Mannie, and it looked like she was mentally trying to put everything into place.

Robin leaned protectively nearer. "She's been through a lot, Mannie."

Mannie ignored her. "Yolanda?"

Yolanda nodded as if the gentle movement hurt. "I remember all of it," she said.

"You happy now?" said Robin.

Mannie pushed ahead. He needed to know and he needed to know sooner rather than later. They may not have a later. "Did you see what Lucas saw? Do you know what Lucas knew?"

Yolanda put on a brave smile. "You're not gonna like it."

Devon stepped out onto the balcony and stood beside Mannie.

"She's asleep," he said.

Mannie placed his hands on the railing, but said nothing. Devon turned and leaned back, looked toward the glass doors.

"The Professor says she's not going to be in any shape to move for some time."

Mannie looked out across the valley, almost as if the answer to all their problems somehow lay out there.

Devon folded his arms. "So, what are we going to do?"

"What choice do we have?"

It was an answer more than a question. Devon took that in, let it sit, then nodded and let out a surrendering sigh.

"So..." he said. He looked at Mannie, but Mannie was still looking out at the valley.

Devon turned around and leaned forward, looked out and tried to see what Mannie saw.

"Okay," he said. "We can't wait for him to *remove us from existence*."

"There's not much doubt about what he meant."

"No. There's not." Devon gripped the rail, looked down at his whitening knuckles.

Karl was standing near the edge of the roof, staring out at the horizon. It was a beautiful day, and after several hours of hard work, he deserved a moment to take stock of his accomplishments.

Mannie came out onto the rooftop, took several slow steps and stopped, realizing Karl wasn't at the workstation. He saw him then, and started toward him. Devon, Carla and the General appeared from the stairwell then and followed him.

As Mannie stepped nearer to Karl, the others moved to either side, spreading out across the roof.

Karl spoke without turning. "Your friend is better?" he asked.

Mannie stopped, still four steps away. He eyed Karl suspiciously.

"A bit."

"That is good."

"She had some interesting things to say."

Karl said nothing at first, continued to look out at the world that was spread out before them. His world…

"Did she?"

"I'm guessing you knew that," said Mannie. When Karl ignored the comment, Mannie continued. "We can't go home."

"I did tell you that, Mr. Alvarez."

"Yes you did. You said that it was because you didn't know where we came from," said Mannie, and he took a step closer. "Now that's not quite true. Is it?"

Karl now did turn about and looked at Mannie. He was calm, almost tranquil. His gaze quickly took in the others standing in a wide semicircle several paces beyond Mannie.

"I have no idea where you come from," he said. "You each come from different worlds, perhaps even from different times."

"That has nothing to do with not being able to send us home."

Karl turned back again to look out at his world. The discussion no longer interested him. "A pleasant evening, is it not?"

"The reason you can't send us home is because home no longer exists."

"Those worlds still exist," he said with a light sigh. "It is Time that has been shattered."

"What does that mean?"

"That is a complex—"

"Dumb it down for me," Mannie said sharply, cutting him off.

Karl turned about smoothly and gave Mannie a thin smile. "My father, the brilliant man that he was, created an interconnecting web consisting of Time and parallel layers of space; a very delicate, very carefully constructed web. My brother, in his ill-conceived attempt to strand me on some half-formed world, destroyed that web. Forever."

Karl looked indifferently at the others of the group, turned his attention back to the colorful horizon, seemingly unconcerned about any possible danger.

"Not his intention, to be sure," he stated.

What a beautiful, beautiful day, he thought.

"Is this where you try to kill me?" he asked. "I should tell you, I am not without defenses."

Devon was several steps behind and to one side of Mannie.

"That had been the plan," he said.

"We find, however, that it will not be necessary," said Mannie.

Karl turned precisely at the unexpected statement. His eyes darted from Devon back to Mannie. He had anticipated something different.

"Is that so?" he asked, for the first time truly curious.

"That is quite so," said the General.

"I see." Karl did not see, though he tried to maintain good form.

Mannie spoke evenly. "Remember that connection your brother established between Yolanda and that system of yours?"

"More accurately, she helped form the bridge between Lucas and the system."

"Whatever."

"That bridge still exists," said Carla.

"Between Yolanda and your machine," said Devon.

Karl smiled thinly. *All is well.* He tapped his temple with a finger.

"I changed the key," he hissed.

"Yeah," said Mannie. "And that would probably mean something if Yolanda wasn't already inside."

Karl's face paled only slightly. He was still trying to maintain control of the situation, but doubt was creeping in.

"Is that so?" he asked, a little less certainly.

"That's so," said Devon.

It took a few moments...
Something... what is that?

A look of confusion washed slowly over Karl's face. He glanced down at the open palm of his right hand. He rubbed his fingers together.

Something is wrong...

He glanced up at Mannie.

Something is wrong...

"No." he mumbled. *Realization…* "Please."

"I'm sorry."

Karl vanished.

There was a brief, hollow sucking sound, and hair and loose clothing were drawn toward the empty space where Karl had been.

Mannie, Devon, Carla and the General were alone on the roof.

Chapter Five

Mannie approached the children's playground at the base of the hillside, the gleaming castle structure towering overhead. He wore a light jacket, a backpack slung over one shoulder, both fairly new.

He came up to Devon and Carla, standing near the swing set. A hundred yards beyond, the General, the Professor, Robin and young Ben were standing in the heart of a patch of freshly turned earth. Robin and Ben were working the soil with shovel and rake. The Professor and the General looked to be doing more discussing and arguing than working.

Devon stepped away from the swing set. "You sure you don't want me to go with you? Only take me five minutes to get my gear together."

"I'll be fine," said Mannie.

"All right, if you're sure. I just hope you're not wasting your time."

Mannie gave a faint shrug. "I know I'll find at least one."

Devon grinned. "You think you can pry her away from that dusty old town?"

"You better," Carla ordered.

"For sure." Devon's grinned broadened. "Mrs. Johansen is the only decent cook in this whole world."

"I'll do my best," said Mannie. His own smile was sad.

"You do that," Carla said, this time more softly. "I'll keep a light on for you."

Mannie looked as though he was going to reach a hand out to Carla, instead shifted the weight of his backpack. "Don't wait up," he said.

Carla reached in close and gave him a light kiss. Mannie looked uncomfortable, but not displeased.

Devon waited for Carla to step back.

"How long you figure you'll be?" he asked.

"Don't really know. But if there are others out there, I need to find 'em. Without the arrivals, they'll be living off the land, what's out there."

"Not possible," stated Devon.

"Exactly."

"Send 'em to us," said Carla.

Mannie appeared ready to go. He glanced over at the group preparing the garden bed.

"Fresh vegetables."

"Eight to twelve weeks, they say," said Devon.

"I might be able to make that."

"We may have stores enough for years—" Carla started.

"—but fresh," Devon finished the thought, "now that's worth coming back for, eh?"

"Absolutely," said Mannie. *There's so little of anything out there.*

The three grew silent. Mannie looked at Devon, then Carla. She again leaned forward and they hugged awkwardly. He turned and shook hands with Devon.

"Don't send us any whackos," said Devon.

"I'll tell 'em the mountains are full of dragons."

Mannie started away. After several steps, he looked ill at ease. He stopped, turned back to the others.

"I never would have let her do that," he said, "if I'd known."

"I don't know that she knew," said Devon.

"I'm sure she's all right, Mannie," said Carla. *Wherever she is...* With Karl? They couldn't know. Not for sure.

"Yeah..."

He started walking again. He looked over at the others toiling in the garden as he passed by.

Robin and Ben stopped their work and waved. The Professor and the General each gave a slight bow.

Epilog

Mannie walked down the center of the dusty street, casually glanced at each building that he passed, looking for any sign of life. The small backpack was strapped to his back; a canteen hung on his belt.

The little town hadn't changed much. Actually, it hadn't changed at all; a handful of weathered buildings with worn, faded siding. He could see his small shack at the end of the row of buildings on his right.

He had the strange sensation of returning home. How odd. He had never thought of this rundown collection of old buildings as home when he lived here. But more than half his time on this world had been spent in this town. He had felt some sense of safety during his time here.

And he hadn't been alone. Here he had found a family of sorts.

He had never thought he needed anyone. He had never been one to have a lot of friends, had never reached out to anyone. But, if pressed on the point, it had been… comfortable… having others nearby, sitting down to dinner with other people… sharing the situation with comrades.

He drifted toward the community hall. He paused only a moment at the foot of the steps, climbed up onto the porch and went inside. He was back out on the porch half a minute later. He stepped onto the top step and looked out at the town. The only movement was dust blowing across the main street.

Mannie appeared to be alone.

He took the steps one at a time, walked down the street to his shack. He left his gear inside his front door, then walked around back and over to the water tank.

It still worked. The running water seemed louder somehow. He washed his face and hands, took a drink, then took the towel and dried his face. He folded the towel neatly and placed it back on its hook.

Mannie stood on the porch of his old shack. He was dressed in fresh, if well-worn clothes. The sky had taken on the dusk colors common to this world. The reds and blues were darker, the shadows murkier.

The town was enveloped in a haunting emptiness.

Mannie's world was a very quiet, very lonely place.

He straightened then, slowly, and looked at a flicker of movement in the distance. As he watched, a silhouette took shape.

Someone was approaching town.

Mannie stepped off the porch and faced the approaching figure. Not until the person was within a hundred yards did Mannie's expression change.

Mrs. Johansen was carrying a large sack over one shoulder. She smiled as she neared, stopped two steps from Mannie and slowly brought sack around off her shoulder and set it down in front of her.

"Good evening, Mrs. Johansen."

"Hello, Mannie," she said. "Good to see you."

"You too." He smiled as he indicated the sack. "D'ya bring me anything?"

Mrs. Johansen reached into the sack, rummaged around and pulled out an orange. She straightened, eyed Mannie, and handed him the orange.

Mannie smelled it appreciatively. There wouldn't be many more of these.

"Very nice. Thanks."

"You're welcome."

Mannie reached down with his free hand and picked up Mrs. Johansen's sack. The two of them walked down the center of the street. A slight breeze blew dust across the scene.

"So, Mrs. Johansen. What are your thoughts regarding carrots?"

"That depends. Cooked or raw?"

"Yes. I suppose that makes a difference, doesn't it?"

"Does to me."

~ End ~